DOUBLE THE D

CAPRICORN COVE SERIES

EVIE MITCHELL

THUNDER THIGHS PUBLISHING

Editor: Nicole Wilson, Evermore Editing

ACKNOWLEDGEMENT OF COUNTRY

I acknowledge the Traditional Custodians of the lands on which I write, the Ngunnawal people, and pay my respect to elders both past and present.

I acknowledge the continued and deep spiritual relationship of the Australian Aboriginal and Torres Strait Islander peoples' to this land, and their unique cultural and spiritual relationships to the land, waters and seas and their rich contribution to society.

Always was, always will be.

*To my husband.
I didn't plan on dedicating this to you but someone
had to win this standoff.*

DOUBLE THE D

Blue

I'd always watched Drake Andrews and Dane Butler from afar. Hotter than hell, I'd fantasised about my Double D's with the kind of kinky need that had Satan engraving my seat in Hell.

When they'd left our small town, I continued to keep track even as I'd breathed a sigh of relief. I couldn't risk revealing just how much I wanted them.

Only now they're back, and that unfortunate fantasy? Well, it's returned—sexier, harder, and hotter than ever.

Drake

Bluebell McKenney has been ours since we stepped into the group home over a decade ago. Her shy glances couldn't hide the heat in her gaze. To have the kind of future we wanted, the kind that involved all three of us, we had to make something of ourselves. But now we're back and ready to claim our woman.

Dane

We weren't meant to practically kidnap her. The plan sure as shit wasn't to become spellbound by her magic breasts. We weren't meant to become lost in her curves or so enamoured by her—er—charms that we forget our own damn names.

Fuck it. The plan may be blown to hell, but one thing's for sure. She's ready for Double the D.

Warning: This MMF is filled with double the entendre, double the fun, and double the you-know-what. Get thee a man (or two) and settle in—this unconventional love story will leave you aching for more.

1

Blue

Dane Butler and Drake Andrews were more like brothers than tangential foster kids who happened to inhabit the same group home. I'd watched them circle each other upon introduction, watched them size each other up and find the other satisfactory.

From afar, I'd watched them merge into one person, becoming closer than blood brothers. They'd ruled our group home, owned our high school, and dominated any sport they'd played. Upon Dane's eighteenth birthday, they'd enrolled in the Marines together, leaving our town in their dust.

Over the last ten years, I'd kept tabs on them

through friends and acquaintances. I knew they were decorated Marines, had settled somewhere close to their training school, and still served together. I'd even heard the whispers about how they did everything together. And when I said everything, I meant *everything*. Something I knew to be a fact, though I'd never admitted it to anyone, let alone myself.

I knew they were back in town. And damn if this newly acquired information wasn't screwing with my equilibrium.

I hid in the canned fruit aisle of the grocery store, gripping a tin of sliced pineapple and blindly staring at the nutritional information as I tried to control my racing heart.

They're back.

I wouldn't have believed it if I hadn't seen them with my own eyes. Hell, when my friend Anika had text me weeks ago I'd assumed she was lying. Or that they were just doing a quick pass through on their way somewhere more interesting.

But nope. They were in the meat aisle, shooting the breeze with old Mr. Henderson.

Breathe, Blue. This will be fine. Totally and completely fine.

Mr. Henderson had lived three doors down from the group home. Growing up, he and his wife had been the kind to hand out candy and offer you a few extra bucks to help them around the house. They'd been incredibly popular with the local kids.

He'd sold the house a year before, moving into a residential care facility. I still visited him twice a week, bringing donuts and coffee in exchange for the gossip he still managed to collect.

Kept this one under your hat, old man. Could have used any information you've collected to prepare for this event. Or, you know, sell my house and move to Australia.

"Pull it together, Blue," I whispered to myself. "You can't leave now. You just need to— suck it up and act like it's not a big deal." I gave myself a mental shake, clearing the cobwebs, and trying to shake off the sudden nerves.

Yep, it is absolutely not a big deal that the two objects of my teenage desire are inhabiting the same space as me. Nope. Not a big deal at all.

I turned, dropping the tin in my cart and pushing further down the aisle. Pride kept me from turning tail and running from the store. If I was lucky, I'd manage to avoid them.

But when am I ever lucky?

I cautiously rounded the corner of the shelving, glancing up and down the next aisle. Three geriatrics and a frazzled mother attempting to pacify a screaming toddler.

Safe.

I turned down the cereal aisle, blindly throwing in three giant boxes of sugar-filled junk, a jar of hazelnut-choc spread, and three loaves of bread. I powered through the rest of my shopping, eyes and ears alert for impending danger.

I hurriedly unloaded at the register, greeting Joan, listening to her chat about the town's latest gossip while I stayed silent, desperate for her hands to move faster as they lifted and scanned the groceries. I tucked the last bag in my cart as Joan rang it up.

"That'll be eighty-three ninety, Hun."

I reached for my wallet, the hair on the back of my neck standing to attention.

Uh-oh—

"Well, if it isn't little Bluebell McKenney." Dane's deep voice sounded abnormally loud in the quiet of the store.

I froze, fingers clutching at my card, a chill racing down my spine.

Caught.

I turned slowly, dread settling like a stone in my stomach. They stood shoulder to shoulder, Dane dark and broody, Drake light with a small smile on his lips. I dropped my gaze, taking in their overflowing cart, heart sinking. That was more food than someone here on holiday required.

It's true. The boys are back in town.

I forced my gaze up, offering what I hoped was a friendly smile while praying the years had buried the memory of our last interaction.

"Dane, Drake. I didn't realise—" I stepped forward, holding out a hand to shake. "Welcome back."

"Come now, Belle," Drake scoffed, his smooth tones a startling contrast to Dane's growl. "Is that any way to greet old friends?" He stepped forward, opening his arms.

I hesitated for a moment, overtly aware of Joan with her gossipy mouth and the interested glances from other shoppers.

I stepped away from the register, closing the distance. As Drake's arms tightened around me, I looked over his shoulder, locking eyes with Dane. His mouth kicked up just a fraction at one corner, satisfaction stamping itself across his face.

The heat and hardness of Drake pressed against me, coupled with Dane's expression, threw me back in time. Back to that night.

Back to—

I pulled back from Drake and shifted toward Dane, offering him the same quick hug and willing myself to keep it together.

"Belle," Dane's words brushed the shell of my ear.

I took a deep breath, memorising the feel of him against me, breathing in the scent of his aftershave and him.

I pulled back, quickly two-stepping away from both of them. I tucked a section of hair behind one ear, fighting overwhelming panic as I moved back to the register.

"Are you in town long?" I turned back to Joan, finally handing her my credit card.

"Bought the Jessup lot. Moved in yesterday."

Dane's low statement had me freezing in place. My head slowly twisted back toward them.

"You bought...." I hadn't heard a whisper about this development.

Why had no one told me?!

It was book club night and my friends, Anika, Collins, Ella and Honey were about to get their asses chewed out.

Ella and Anika co-owned the town's best (and currently only) bar. Collins worked with Honey at the local physiotherapist and wellness centre, and I worked as a nurse in the local clinic. Between the five of us we generally had our fingers on the gossip pulse.

Not so much it seemed.

"That's... wow." I said finally, unsure how to continue. "Congratulations."

"Thanks. We finally got out. Decided it was time to do something different."

"And you...." My tongue felt too big for my mouth. "You're going to run a kid's summer camp?"

They both chuckled. "Nah, we're setting up a wilderness retreat. Scuba diving, hiking, that kind of thing."

"People pay for that?" The words tumbled out of my mouth before I could stop them. My cheeks warmed; hands now clammy.

"Megabucks, sweetheart," Drake said in a fake whisper. "Gods bless their city asses."

Behind them, a woman cleared her throat. "Why, if it isn't Drake and Dane. Welcome back."

Hannah Sharp had ruled our high school with cutting words, perfect blonde hair, and heels that would easily crush you if she so chose. While some of us had left high school behind upon graduation, it seemed that the Ice Queen's reign continued.

While she distracted Dane and Drake, I paid for my things, making a break for the exit.

"Have a nice day, Blue," Joan called, turning to start her slow scan of the men's items.

I lifted my hand in farewell, ignoring the itch of awareness between my shoulder blades.

Please, God, let me never see them again.

In a town this size? My wish was as likely to be granted as Mr. Henderson was to walk on the moon.

Damn.

My phone buzzed with a text.

BOOKISH BITCHES CHAT
ELLA

ZOMG! You spoke to them!

BLUE

You SAWWWWWW?????

ELLA

I'm literally in the cereal aisle right now trying to negotiate with Gunnar about oats. OF COURSE I SAW.

ANIKA

What are we talking about?

HONEY

Wait. By them do you mean *THEM*?????

COLLINS

Oh shit! As in the two dashing me we all want to be in a love sandwich with?

ELLA

Except me. One Viking is enough

ANIKA

Gags

Seconded in the safety of my car, I hesitated, my thumbs hovering over the keyboard

BLUE

Alas, yes. And it was as awkward as expected. I'm about to go home and drown myself in a tub of cookie dough ice cream and humiliation.

ANIKA

How bad are we talking?

BLUE

I had to be rescued by Hannah.

HONEY

Ouch. You know, Hannah is okay when you get to know her. A little standoffish and next to no idea of how to speak to people, but she's not bad.

COLLINS

Less about Hannah and more about Blue, babe.

HONEY

Sorry. Okay, Blue, I'm sure it wasn't that bad.

I thumbed my head against the steering wheel of my car, replaying my stumbling, stuttering nonsense.

BLUE

It was. Kill me.

ELLA

No one is killing anyone. First meetings are always weird. Now you can move on. And get to the good stuff.

ANIKA

You mean anal? Blue does strike me as the type. My advice? Plenty of lube. Those two guys do not look like they'd be small.

HONEY

OMG! ANIKA!

COLLINS

You went there. You really went there.

ELLA

Ani... how many times do I have to tell you that anal is not something you just spring in a group?

Chuckling, I tossed my text on my passenger seat and started my car.

"Next time will be better."

2

Dane

"We let her slip right through our fucking fingers," Drake bemoaned our situation for the fifteenth time in as many minutes. "Why did we let Hannah Sharp talk for so long? Hannah fucking Sharp."

I kept silent. I'd long since learned the best way to deal with Drake was to let him get his bitching out.

"So," he said, handing me a length of looped rope. "What's the plan?"

I hung the rope on the wall, then made a note in the safety program on our tablet. We were starting from scratch with this adventure tourism gig. Everything had to be perfect before we even considered signing up customer number one.

Not that I was worried. Twelve years in the Marines had taught us both to be prepared for any situation, and the old ranch was perfectly positioned for this venture.

We'd purchased the parcel of cleared land where reformed city slickers had once tried to run a small herd of cattle—it hadn't exactly worked out for them. But the ranch was surrounded by the mountains of the national park to the east and the coastline to the west.

We were about a twenty-minute drive from town and less than that to some great wineries and farm-to-plate restaurants. The house itself sat on an elevated part of the block. For all their foolishness, the former owners had done an excellent job of building what could only be described as a beach-meets-farm. Six bedrooms, three bathrooms, multiple living areas, a basement, an attic, and a library, were all offset by a giant porch that looked out over the ocean. I'd taken one walk around the house and made an offer on the property.

We'd already submitted the required plans and permissions to the county for approval for our resort. We planned to have year-round eco-lodges available and couple that with adventure and wilderness activities. We planned to be all-terrain all the time. Now we were just waiting for the damn council members to pull their fucking fingers out so we could get the building started. In the meantime, we'd run our tour business, taking rich assholes out to climb mountains and paddle canoes and feel like real men for once in their lives.

Though I'd be leaving the customer service to Drake.

"The plan?" Drake prompted again.

I saved the additions in the program, shutting down the tablet and tucking it under my arm. "We track her down."

I'd already put a call into Mr. Henderson.

"And?"

"We convince her to give us a chance." I let my stoicism slip just a fraction, the anticipation getting the better of me. "And based on her reaction in the store yesterday, I don't expect that'll be hard."

Drake shifted, running a hand over his crotch. "No," he agreed. "Did you see those nipples?"

I had. Her reaction to us had been instantaneous. The flush, the brief flash of desire, her pulse fluttering madly at her neck.

You'll be ours soon, Baby.

"But damn," Drake continued. "If I'm not hard as a fucking stone in the meantime."

I lifted an eyebrow. "You asking for somethin'?"

He grinned, spreading his arms wide in welcome. "Only if you're offering."

"Back against the wall, unzip."

Drake backed up, that sly grin now permanently fixed on his face. Leaning against the wall, his big hands dropped to his fly. He paused, drawing the moment out, letting me know he wasn't so easily controlled.

Oh, just wait.

He shifted, hands going up to pull his shirt off. He tossed it aside, dropping his hands back to his crotch.

I raised an eyebrow, crossing my arms. "Did I tell you to take that off?"

His grin was quick and dirty. "As if you're not interested in seeing this." He slid a hand down his abs, hooking it into the front of his jeans.

"You need to learn patience," I told him, not moving an inch.

"And you need to learn how to give in," he returned, fingers now pulling at his fly. He lowered the zipper, peeling his jeans and briefs down his legs. He paused for a second, pulling off his boots and socks before rising, arms outstretched in welcome.

"Like what you see?"

I let my gaze drift slowly over his body. Hard muscle, skin tan from hours in the sun, a few scars—all of which I knew intimately. Drake had long limbs, a lean body, and a cock that stood heavy and hard.

"You'll do," I drawled, knowing my lack of reaction would drive him crazy. We played this game over and over; sometimes he won, and sometimes I did. But either way, we both got off.

"Fuck you," Drake dropped his arms, one hand dropping to stroke his long cock. "Come suck me, you dirty fucker."

I moved to him, slow and deliberate. My cock pressed against the fly of my jeans, my body hard and hot. I pushed his hand aside, gripping his shaft tightly in my fist.

"You want something," I told him, giving his cock a vicious stroke. "You ask nicely."

Drake groaned, slumping back against the wall, his hips thrusting helplessly into my hold.

"Suck me," he told me, breathless and desperate.

I stopped stroking. "Say, please."

"Fuck you."

I grinned, enjoying this back and forth, knowing it turned us both the fuck on.

I pushed out a sad sigh. "Guess you don't want—"

His hand shot out, covering mine, forcefully keeping my fingers around his cock.

"Please," he gritted out, jaw clenched.

I made a tutting sound in the back of my throat, leaning close to nip him on his collarbone. "Please, what?"

"Please, Dane. Suck me."

Instead, I fisted his hair, pulling him close and smashing our mouths together. We fought for dominance, his hands wrapping around me to battle for control. I jerked him between us, our bodies sliding together—mine fully clothed, his naked. I knew the difference would drive him higher.

"Do it," he barked, reaching down to cup my cock through my jeans. "Fucking suck me."

I slid hungry lips down his body as I slowly lowered to the ground, sucking and nipping, tasting the salt of his skin as I made my way down. On my knees, I fisted his cock, bringing it to my mouth. I paused, glancing up, seeing him looking down at me with half-mast eyes.

"You know Belle is gonna cream the first time she sees me doing this to you," I muttered, giving him a small jerk.

My words, deliberately chosen, were enough to tip Drake over the edge. He fisted my hair, pulling me onto his cock, thrusting until he hit the back of my throat. I revelled in his loss of control, my hands coming up to grip his ass, letting him thrust into my mouth with wild abandon.

"Fuck, Dane. Fuck. Baby," Drake held my head, pressing deep into the back of my throat as he came. I swallowed, sucking it down.

"Shit," he muttered, releasing his grip and sagging against the wall. "Fuck, that was hot."

I wiped at the corner of my mouth, grinning as I stood. "Give me a second, and I'll—"

"Nah," I muttered, readjusting my crotch. "I'm good for now."

Drake raised an eyebrow, giving my pants a meaningful look. A quick glance revealed that my jeans were doing jack shit to hide my massive erection.

"I'll fuck you later tonight," I told him, unafraid of a case of blue balls. "We gotta go."

Drake reached down, casually pulling his jeans up his long legs. "Where?"

"Mr. Henderson." I grinned, anticipation tingling at the base of my spine. "We've got a woman to claim."

❦

DRAKE DROVE while I called our flaky boat builder.

"Look, I get you guys want this done. But the

fact is, I can't meet your impossible deadline. You gotta work with me here," Simon whined.

I exchanged a glance with Drake, my mouth thinning into an unimpressed line. He rolled his eyes before looking back at the road.

"Simon, we told you six months ago our deadline. You assured us you'd have the crew ready to go when we settled here. Our specifications for this build aren't unusual. If you can't meet our deadline, we'll find someone who can."

He huffed and puffed and tried to wheedle me into a compromise. Fact was, we needed this guy to start the project now. We were heading into winter, and unless he started it over this period, there was no way the boat would be ready for spring/summer next year. The boat would seat up to fifty tourists and would be equipped with a catering area, toilets, and storage for all our various gear.

"No," I finally snapped as Drake turned into the nursing home complex. "We're terminating this contract. I expect our deposit to be returned by next week."

"But—"

"You signed an airtight contract. You can't deliver by our agreed date; we have every right to pull out," I informed the sorry excuse for a human being. "My lawyer will be in touch."

I hit end, blowing out a breath.

"We gonna be able to find another builder?" Drake asked lightly.

"Give me a week. If we can't, we'll start looking at alternatives. Maybe buy something cheap to tide us over."

That was the worst-case scenario. We wanted to start this enterprise exactly right. No cutting corners, no second-hand purchases. We needed to be taken seriously in order to attract the kind of clientele we wanted—rich corporate types ready to splash the cash for a little thrill. This was why we were giving ourselves a full six months to get everything settled.

That, and six months would be a nice fucking chunk of time to woo Belle. Though I didn't expect it would take quite that long.

"Oh, shit," Drake murmured as he pulled to a stop in front of Mr. Henderson's small unit. "Isn't that Belle's car?"

Sure enough, in Mr. Henderson's tiny driveway was the same navy blue, no-nonsense Impala that we'd witnessed speeding out of the grocery store's car park yesterday—Belle's pale face tight with anxiety at the wheel.

"Well," I drawled, unsnapping my seat belt. "Ain't this a nice surprise."

"Fucking jackpot," Drake agreed.

We exited the car into the sultry late afternoon. Autumn had settled, but we were experiencing a late heat spell—complete with a crackling storm the night before. Despite the wind and lightning's best efforts, our little farmhouse had stood strong. Clean-up had only been a few branches this morning.

Drake hurried to the door, hitting the bell.

"Settle, bro," I murmured, clasping his shoulder. "We don't want a repeat of yesterday."

Drake took a steadying breath, then nodded. "Slow and easy."

Mr. Henderson pulled the door open, beaming as he ushered us in. "Boys! Come in, come in. I didn't expect to see you so soon."

We'd reconnected in the grocery store. The old guy had been our lifeline these past few years, slipping us intel on Belle, what she was up to, who she was dating. Hell, even before we'd shipped out, he'd been looking out for us. The old man had overpaid us for maintaining his garden and car. He'd been the one to suggest we look at the Marines as an option. Hadn't hurt that he'd served and gave us all the gory but enticing details.

We stepped through, allowing him to wrap us in back-clapping hugs. Mrs. Henderson had passed two years ago. It was part of the reason why we'd decided to call it quits. Time was passing, and we'd been overseas, unable to return in time for the funeral.

We were fucking good at our jobs. Enjoyed the shit out of the travel and adventure. Fuck, even the regimented schedule hadn't been that bad. But we weren't getting younger, and we knew Belle wanted kids. Mr. Henderson had told us she'd stepped up her dating game, trying to snag herself a man. It had taken us two years to transition out, but now we were ready. Ready for her.

"Good to see you," I muttered, accepting his hug.

"You're just in time. Belle just arrived, and I've put a fresh pot of coffee on. Come join us."

He led us down a hall that had three bright pink suitcases leaning neatly against the wall. "Ignore the mess; Belle's staying here for a few days." I glanced at Drake, finding his gaze already on me. He lifted an eyebrow, a small satisfied grin settling on his face.

Minuscule and clinical, the unit was nothing like the homely house Mr. Henderson had lived in before. Oh sure, there were pictures hung, while photos and knickknacks sat scattered about on display. But underneath, the place felt like a hospital room masquerading as a home.

I exchanged a look with Drake. He nodded,

his normally jovial expression completely wiped from his face.

For a man we cared so deeply about, this was unacceptable.

We entered the kitchen and found Belle standing at the sink, chopping vegetables.

"Look who I found," Mr. Henderson called, moving to settle in one of the chairs.

Belle glanced over her shoulder, an easy smile ready on her face. As she registered our presence, that smile froze. Her body tensed, the knife falling silent. Her eyes widened until she looked a little like a deer in headlights.

"Belle," Drake grinned, heading over to her. "We have to keep meeting like this." He quickly removed the knife from her hand, dropping it to the counter and then wrapped her in a hug.

I watched, satisfaction building as her cheeks coloured. Drake kept her wrapped in his arms just a beat too long, and I watched, anticipation unfurling, when she didn't protest.

Drake let her go, one hand resting on the small of her back, propelling her toward me. "Go greet, Dane."

She complied, coming to me, and letting me wrap her in a hug. Good girl. I breathed her in. She smelled like lemongrass and home. Our girl felt fucking fantastic in my arms. Her curves were deliciously generous and perfectly plump.

Her Double-D tits pressed against me, and I couldn't help the rumble of pleasure that echoed in my chest.

Her breath caught, and her body trembled once before she stepped back. She immediately looked away, hand reaching up to tuck stray hairs behind her ear.

"I...I-I-I didn't realise you were coming today," she finally stammered, standing awkwardly in the middle of the small kitchenette.

"Thought we'd drop by and see our main man," Drake said, sliding easily onto one of the seats at the four-seater table. He clasped a hand on Mr. Henderson's shoulder. "Gotta make up for lost time."

Her hands lifted, fluttering up to touch her collarbone before settling on her hips. "Right. Well, I'll just get back to dinner." She turned, hesitating. "Did you want to stay?"

The words were a concession. Everyone in the room except old Mr. Henderson knew how much it cost her.

"Love to, Honey," I answered for us. "Whatcha making?"

"Chicken biryani."

"Sounds great. Can we help?"

She blinked. "Um, no. But thank you."

I settled on the opposite side of Mr. Henderson while he dished out coffee, donuts, and the latest gossip. Sally and Johnny were divorced. The old Randall couple had sold up and moved to Idaho to be closer to their grandkids. Belle's parents, the people who'd run the group home, were in Europe for the summer. The Stones' and Bronze's were still locked in a battle for the cabins up new Lover's Lake.

"And what about our fine little Bluebell?" Drake asked, leaning back in his chair. "What's been happening with you, Miss Belle?"

She'd been quietly frying and chopping in the background, the smells teasing my taste buds. She stiffened, the knife stilling.

"It's Blue now," she murmured, still turned away from us.

"Sorry?"

She cleared her throat, shoulders straightening. She twisted, giving us a serious look. "I go by Blue."

I sensed from her tone that this was important to her. "Any particular reason for the change?"

She gestured down at her body. "Bluebell is the name of some white girl wearing Daisy duke cut-offs and a crop top. That's never gonna be me."

"Baby, you can wear cut-offs and crop tops around us any time," I told her, letting everyone in the room hear the heat in my voice.

But I got it. No one had believed two punk kids could make it. Only Bluebell's great aunt on her daddy's side had stood by them. She'd been named for that aunt, but it had to be admitted it was one of the frilliest names I'd ever heard.

"Blue," I muttered, liking the taste of her name on my tongue. Liking even more her little shiver of pleasure. "Okay, Blue it is."

She nodded once, then returned to the stove, swirling a large spoon through the simmering curry. "Nothing to really add. I'm sure Mr. Henderson has told you everything."

He had, but so had her parents. In dribs and drabs over the last decade, we'd received updates on little Miss Blue. She'd worked two jobs while studying nursing, then landed a job in the hospital a town over. After a few years there, she'd transferred to a local clinic, preferring the short commute and friendlier hours. When Mrs. Henderson had passed and Mr. Henderson had moved into aged care, she'd helped him sell the house, pack up his things, and move in here.

"Ah, pish-posh." Mr. Henderson shook his head. "Blue's roof got damaged in the storm last night. She's staying with me."

As one, Drake and I turned to look at the beautiful woman in the kitchen. "What about your parent's house?"

"They're renting it out while in Europe."

Three years ago, her mother had a health scare. The lump turned out to be benign, but it'd left the family changed. We'd still been deployed but had heard all about it. Mr. and Mrs. McKenney had continued to assist the current kids in their care. Once the kids were settled—either with a family or in their own digs—the McKenney's travelled.

They'd taken on so many difficult kid cases—me and Drake included—that no one could begrudge them this alone time.

"But this is a one-bedroom unit," Drake's tone was deceptively casual. "Where you gonna sleep?"

"The sofa bed. I tried to get a room, but it's peak tourist season." She raised a shoulder in a shrug, her back still to us.

"Couldn't stay with friends?"

She flushed, brushing nervously at the strands of hair that wisped across her cheeks.

"They're either on vacation, have a full house, or don't have a spare bed. It's summer break, so—" she trailed off.

"You know, we got a few spare bedrooms," I drawled, deceptively casual. "We could always put you up."

"And we're closer to the clinic," Drake added helpfully.

"Boys, that's a mighty fine idea." Mr. Henderson raised his coffee mug in a salute. "There you go, Blue. No need to lose sleep on that lumpy couch."

Oh, she'll still be losing sleep.

I picked up a donut and shoved it in my mouth, concentrating on chewing rather than giving in to the overwhelming need to press her against the closest flat surface and taste her.

"I couldn't." She'd abandoned the stove to stand at the kitchen counter, wiping over and over the same spot.

"Why not?" Drake asked, smiling at her. "We got the rooms; you need a place. You're not even unpacked."

She looked panicked. "I promised Mr. Henderson I'd drive him to the—"

"Oh, nonsense," Mr. Henderson fluttered a hand dismissively. "I can drive myself just like I've done every other time." He glanced at me, rolling his eyes. "Due for a check-up." He tapped a hand over his heart. "Need to get the old ticker checked. No need to worry, just making sure everything is as it should be."

"But—" Blue protested.

"Darling, I appreciate your support. But you sleeping on my couch isn't going to work for either of us. Take the boys' generous offer and get yourself some much-needed rest."

She bit her lip, looking down at her feet. I waited, not moving, not even daring a glance at Drake.

Say yes. Say yes.

"Okay." She blew out a breath. "The insurance guy will be around tomorrow. It should only be for a week at the most." She glanced from me to Drake. "Is that okay?"

"Baby," I leaned back in my chair, triumph and satisfaction settling in my chest. "You can stay forever."

Her cheeks flushed, and she fumbled with the wooden spoon in her hand, turning back to the stovetop. "I don't think that'll be necessary."

I glanced over at Drake. He shot me a look, eyes dark with desire, a hungry grin across his lips.

Oh, yeah. This was going to be fun.

3

Blue

I couldn't fall asleep. The bed in Dane and Drake's guest room felt like a cloud. The linen smelled fresh, and the pillows were deliciously luxurious.

But I still couldn't sleep.

They'd practically kidnapped me from Mr. Henderson's. After dinner, they'd washed and dried the dishes, then cleaned the kitchen, telling me to sit and relax. They'd served up coffee and tea, cleaned and put away the dishes, then whisked my luggage into their car. Drake chauffeured me in their SUV back to the Jessup —wait, no—back to *their* property while Dane had followed in my little car.

I'd felt weirdly on edge the whole time. I

knew I shouldn't. I'd lived with these men for four years. I'd been fourteen when they'd arrived in the house—angry sixteen-year-olds, too full of piss and vinegar to want to have anything to do with the other kids. They'd pushed every boundary, fought every rule, argued with my parents until they'd finally realized my daddy wasn't one for budging. Tough love from him, silk over steel from my Mumma.

My parents had taken in kids no one wanted. Pregnant teens with screaming babies, damaged children from broken homes, teens with eyes too old and burning anger at the world. All types had passed through our doors. I had one blood sister and one blood brother, but hundreds of siblings by association.

Drake and Dane were the only "siblings" I'd ever wanted to sleep with. And it's strange, but I only ever viewed them as a package deal—I couldn't love one without the other.

The hot flush of embarrassment crept up my neck, heating my cheeks. I groaned, draping one arm over my eyes as I remembered that night.

I'd stood in the shadows of the garage, hands pressed against the weatherboard, the wood scratching at my palms, my breathing ragged as sixteen-year-old me watched Dane and Drake make out in the back seat of Drake's car.

Drake had turned eighteen three months before, and I knew they were both waiting for Dane's birthday before they left our house. My Mumma and Daddy weren't ones for turning out kids on their eighteenth birthday, but these boys were ready. They'd been adults for a long time.

They'd returned from a night out, celebrating Dane's birthday. I'd heard them roll in, the car sliding into the garage, then silence. They hadn't come barreling in, sneaking up the stairs as they normally did.

We'd celebrated earlier that day. A fancy lunch my parents had organised for Dane. I'd helped decorate the cake. The kids had all sung happy birthday while Dane glowered—as per his usual expression. My Mumma had showered him with kisses and hugs, getting teary when she retold the story of Dane's arrival at our house and his subsequent transformation into a man of quality.

"No boys reside in my house," my Mumma had declared. "Only men of quality."

Dane's façade had chipped just a little at her proclamation. My daddy had agreed, describing his pride in Dane, and I'd watched, entirely too aware of the way Drake draped an arm around his foster brother, giving him strength.

They'd taken the car, disappearing after the festivities. The phone had rung, a foster agency desperate for someone to help with an emergency case.

My parents had packed up, springing into action. They'd left an hour ago, and I knew they wouldn't return until the early hours.

"Lock the door, Corazón," my mother had called as she'd double-checked her purse. "The fratres will be home in a few hours. Watch the bebes."

I'd stayed awake, restlessly pacing. Besides Drake and Dane, there was only me, my two younger siblings, and one foster toddler in the house. All of whom were sleeping soundly. I'd wanted to go with the boys. I'd wanted to sit in the backseat while they gave each other shit, teasing and laughing. They revolved around each other, circling closer until, in my mind, it became nearly impossible to separate Drake from Dane. They were joined, two parts of the same whole, and I loved being around them.

Curious that it had been nearly ten minutes since their arrival, I went to investigate—finding more than I bargained for.

"Yeah," Drake's groan broke the silence of the garage. "Like that."

Dane's quiet chuckle sounded low and rough. Dirtier, hotter than the rare times I'd heard it over the dinner table.

"This?" Dane asked, his voice teasing.

Drake swore in response.

"Or this?" A long, loud moan filled the garage.

I shuddered, knowing I shouldn't be here.

Knowing I shouldn't be hiding in the shadows, listening to their private moment. It didn't help that I couldn't see much beyond their shadowy outline through the car's rear window. Their bodies moving, heaving, their hands hidden from my view.

"Fuck," Drake grunted. "I need to come."

"Nuh-uh. It's my birthday. Pretty sure I get to decide who comes and when." There was a slight pause. "And where."

"Fuck." I watched Drake fist his fingers in Dane's hair, pulling him down to fuse their mouths together.

They moved together now, their bodies fighting for dominance even as they enjoyed the dance. My fingers fisted in the hem of my sleep shirt, my body heavy and damp with need. Hot, sticky wet coated that secret part of me, slicking my thighs with need.

"Fuck, baby." It was Dane's turn to groan. "Yeah, fist it. Harder. Make me ache."

I wanted to see. The thought lodged itself in my brain, unable to be swayed. I wanted to see this. Them. I wanted to watch as they came.

I took one step, my bare foot carefully, silently, landing against the concrete floor.

Five more steps, that's all it would take for me to be close enough to them, close enough to see through the window as they did things my mind had only ever wondered about.

They grunted, swore, and praised each other as

I stepped closer, my hands finding the cool metal of the car.

Under my hands, the car rocked, shifting from one side to the other as I lifted on tip-toe, my breath catching at the beauty before me.

Dane and Drake were fisting each other's cocks, one hand on the other's cock, the other clenched in hair or shirt. Brutally they jerked, their lips almost brutal as they gasped for more.

I'd never seen a more beautiful sight than this.

"Fuck," Drake pulled back, his head dropping onto Dane's chest, his eyes clenched tight as he came. They panted in the aftermath, their hands roaming. Dane's hips twitched as he lightly humped the air.

"Shit, sorry," Drake muttered, his hand dropping back to Dane's cock. "Your turn, birthday boy."

He jerked Dane's cock hard and fast. I watched, enthralled, my breath lightly fogging the glass. One jerk, two, three. They smashed their lips together as Dane came, his head dropping to Drake's shoulder, teeth nipping through the t-shirt into skin as he grunted through his release.

"That's it, baby," Drake encouraged. "Come all over me."

Dane collapsed against Drake's body. Their arms wrapped around each other, quiet filling the garage once again.

I tried to control my breathing. My body was

flushed with need, hot desire flowing through every part of me. My breasts felt heavy, my breathing ragged.

The boys slowly drew apart.

"Come on, better check on the kids."

Shit.

I made a dash for the door. I would have made it too, if not for the broom handle. My balance was immediately thrown off, my foot flying out from under me as the handle rolled under my foot. I slipped, landing awkwardly on my side, smacking into the concrete with a hard crack.

"Belle!" They were there, hands gently turning me, faces still flushed, clothes and hair rumpled. My face flushed, mortified that I'd interrupted their moment.

"I'm fine," I muttered, pulling away from their gentle hands. "Just tripped, is all."

"Why aren't you in bed?" Drake demanded as I pushed to my feet.

I lifted one shoulder in a shrug, ignoring the shooting pain the movement caused.

"She's sixteen. It's a weekend, and only just gone two. She's being a normal fucking teenager, you idiot," Dane said, giving Drake an eye-roll. He turned to me. "But, babe, you're gonna have to explain why you were in the garage running away from our car at this time of night."

I froze, unable to make my mouth form the words.

Drake blew out a long breath, a hand running through his hair. "You saw."

I bit my lip, the heat on my cheeks betraying any denials I may have considered uttering.

They both fell silent, watching me and then glancing at each other in silent communication.

"We're bi," Drake finally said. "Swing both ways."

"So, you're—what?" I whispered, hugging my arms to myself.

They both chuckled. "Let's just say nothing we feel for each other is brotherly."

"We're together," Dane told me.

"Oh." I didn't know what to say. Congratulations? Happy life? How can I be a part of your coupledom?

Dane narrowed his eyes. "You liked what you saw, babe?"

Every single part of my body froze at the question. Their gazes were on me, hot and wanting. Desire rocketed through my veins, every inch of me hyper-aware of them.

I couldn't force the words out. Couldn't work out how to tell them they were beautiful together. That they were perfect, and I wanted to be a part of that perfection.

"She liked it," Drake answered for me. "Her body wants us."

"But does her mind?" Dane asked, taking a step closer. "Do you, Belle?"

"Yes," I whispered, caught in their undertow. "I want both of you."

As one, they reached for me, pulling me to them. A mouth caught mine in a kiss, and another landed on my neck, licking and sucking.

I hadn't believed this could be real. That they could feel as passionately about me as I felt about them.

"How?" I panted. "How is this happening?"

"Babe, it was only a matter of time."

I fell into them, letting them lead. Letting them guide me.

"Fuck, she's sixteen," Dane muttered, pressing another needy kiss to my swollen lips. "I'm sorry, Belle, but we can't—" he broke off, kissing me with abandon.

"We won't do anything," Drake promised, his voice harsh even as his hands gently palmed my butt. "Just play a little—"

Outside, a car crunched up the gravel of our driveway. We froze, locked together in an intimate embrace.

The garage door made a sound of protest, and we immediately moved. Drake snatched my hand

and pulled me after him, Dane's hand on my back as we ran for the stairs. Up into the house, across the living areas, and up the stairs toward our bedrooms.

They paused at my door.

"We're leaving, Belle," Drake told me in a hurried whisper. "Maybe tomorrow, maybe a month. But we're heading out. Gotta make something of ourselves."

"But we'll be back," Dane promised, one hand coming up to caress my cheek. "We'll come back to you."

The sound of my parent's muted voices and movements floated up the staircase.

"I love you," I whispered. "Both of you."

They grinned but still stepped back.

"Wait for us, pretty girl."

It had taken a month between them first signing up and finally leaving for boot camp. A month of awkward interactions at the dining table. Of heated glances and lingering touches. Of stolen kisses in dark corners.

And then they left, and there was—nothing. No phone calls or emails. Each year they'd send a birthday card and a gift. But otherwise—nothing. They didn't return while on leave. They'd never referenced our moment together again.

And I'd grown tired of waiting for something, of wanting something that I was convinced would never happen.

Are you sure it'll never happen? That insidious little voice broke through the cloud of memories. *Yes,* I told my inner voice firmly. *They're a couple. They don't need me.*

But they want you.

Not anymore.

Are you sure?

My phone beeped with an incoming text.

HONEY

Sorry again about the lack of bed space. If it's really bad I can set up the tent and kick my cousins out.

I grinned at Honey's text.

BLUE

It's fine. Honestly, it's almost like being back at my parents.

HONEY

Now that I don't believe. Those two men are fine as fuck. If it were me, I'd be running through that house naked until one of them pounced.

BLUE

No pouncing going on here. Just them being nice.

HONEY

Hmm… I'll believe that when I
see it.

I sighed, pushing off the blankets and getting to my feet. At this rate, sleep felt like a long way off.

May as well make some tea and find a book to read.

I crept through the quiet house, enjoying the soothing colours and warm tones of the wood and stone. The boys had done an amazing job decorating—pairing unique souvenirs from their travels with comfortable furnishings.

I had a feeling Drake was behind the decorating. The man had always liked to create spaces he could describe as home.

In the kitchen, I lifted the kettle, moving to the sink to fill it, when a sound drifted from the lounge. I froze, fear surging through me.

"Fuck, yeah," a voice whispered in the dark.

I silently replaced the kettle on the counter, tip-toeing down the hall to the lounge. Just beside the doorway, I paused, ears straining as I waited for the sound to come again.

"You gonna make me wait?" Drake's voice demanded in the dark.

"Blue's not ours yet," Dane replied.

"Bastard."

I heard sounds like wrestling, clothes moving, the slap of skin against skin, the hot wet slick of mouths sucking.

My eyes drifted shut, hope surging at their whispers. This reality was hotter, wetter, dirtier.

There's no one to stop us.

We were ten, nearly eleven years older. Wiser. Out of the home, living our own lives.

They've been gone for a long time.

I wanted to walk around the corner. I wanted to stand in the doorway and let them peel my clothes from my body. I wanted them to—

"You're gonna come." Drake's harsh demand interrupted my fantasy. "You need it."

"No. I want to come on Blue," Dane replied, his voice strangled.

"It may be a long wait, babe. Let me at least give you some relief."

"But—" Dane's groan ended any protests he may have voiced. "Hate you."

"Nah, you fucking love me."

"Yeah, but I'm still gonna fight you."

"Counting on it."

I heard them move, the sounds more frantic, more needy, just—more.

And I needed to see.

I stepped into the opening, nearly gasping at the sight before me.

Men. Skin. Muscles. Sweat. Beauty.

They were beautiful. So damn beautiful it hurt to look at them. Their bodies were muscular perfection. The warm glow of the lamp in the room highlighted the plains and dips of their bodies.

They were naked, their clothes scattered about. Drake straddled Dane, their hands and mouths all over each other.

"You gonna watch or join in?"

I jolted, eyes flying to see Dane watching at me over Drake's shoulder.

I opened my mouth, unsure how to answer.

"What?" Drake asked, shooting me a look that was pure devilry. "Cock got your tongue?"

"In," the word was a bare whisper.

They both froze.

"Say it again," Dane demanded.

"In." I cleared my throat. "I want to join you. Both of you."

They moved, Drake rolling off Dane, both surging to their feet. They strode to me, cocks proud and heavy. My mouth watered with the possibility. I wanted—

Everything.

Their hands landed on me, stripping my clothes from my body. Dressed only in the soft lamplight, I stood before them, wondering if they cared about the curves and abundance of my body. I'd always been overly curvy. Hips and ass, breasts and belly. My mother encouraged me to embrace my beauty, taught me to dress for it, and raised me up knowing that every woman is a goddess and beautiful in her own way.

It didn't stop the small seed of doubt sprouting as they gazed at my naked skin.

"Beautiful," Drake whispered reverently.

"Worth every fucking second of the long wait," Dane agreed.

My hands fluttered, needing something to hold on to, needing something to keep me grounded.

"Here, baby," Drake whispered, getting close. He picked up my hand, placing it across his chest. On my other side, Dane did the same.

Under my palms, I felt their hearts beat. The reassuring heat of their bodies warmed my hands, wrapping me in a fog of neediness.

"You ready, baby?" Dane asked, his voice low and soft.

I tilted my face toward him, offering a small smile. "Yes."

My words untethered the leash holding them back. As one, they reached for me, hands grazing my skin.

"Kiss her," Drake barked out, his head descending to my breast.

Dane chuckled, pulling me a step closer to him, fingers weaving in my hair.

"Been craving another taste of you, Blue." His whispered admission left me shivering. "We spent many nights getting each other off to the thought of you."

Drake's mouth closed around my breast, and I gasped, eyes closing, head falling back.

Dane's hand tilted my head toward him, his lips capturing mine in a greedy kiss. He deepened it, immediately teasing my tongue with his.

And just like that, I jumped headfirst into the wildest experience of my life.

4

Drake

Watching my boyfriend kiss our girlfriend, but-she-hasn't-admitted-it-yet was hotter than fuck. I pulled back, regretfully letting her nipple fall from my lips, shifting to give them space. Blue pressed against Dane, their mouths meeting over and over in hungry rapture.

I'd always assumed I'd experience jealousy in this moment, watching the two most important people in my life making out without me. Happily, I felt nothing but satisfaction. Well, that and horny. Fuck, my cock jutted out, rigid and ready. Pre-cum glistened on my tip. I ran a hand over it, collecting the wet and dragging it down my cock, jerking on my hard length.

Fuck, they were beautiful. Dane gripped Blue's thick thighs, boosting her up, wrapping her legs around his hips, and walking the three steps to push her back against the wall. She whimpered, shifting against him, her hands clutching at his back, threading through his hair.

Dane dropped his head, sucking on her neck. Blue's eyelids fluttered open, her eyes locking with mine, flaring as they took in me stroking my cock.

"You like me watching you, little Blue?" I asked, tightening my grip and giving a harder jerk. Her lips parted, gaze locked on my cock.

"Dane," I drawled. "You wanna move this to the bedroom?" Dane, never one to be rushed, continued to kiss her neck.

"He's not listening," Blue told me, a grin lighting her face.

"Oh," Dane lifted his head. "I am. Just finding it hard to stop tasting you."

I chuckled, dropping my cock and striding across the room. I slid a hand up Dane's back, over his shoulder, and reached across to cup Blue's jaw. "But imagine all the other places we can taste." Dane shifted Blue a little higher, turning for the door. "Good point."

He started down the hall, Blue letting out a startled shriek.

"Dane! Let me down! You'll hurt yourself."

"Babe," I laughed, following them. "You're not that heavy."

"Have you seen me?" she asked horrified. "I'm big and—"

"Don't finish that sentence. Don't you even fucking think about it," Dane barked, entering our bedroom.

He dropped her gently on the bed, backing up to stand beside me. "You're beautiful. Fucking perfect."

She pushed up on one elbow, her cheeks flushed. "You don't have to—"

"Jesus, Bluebell. Stop it. We love you. Every single part of you." I glanced over at Dane, letting out a long sigh. "Guess we're just gonna have to show her." Dane shot me a grin. "After you."

I advanced, dropping to my knees at the end of the bed and dipping my head to kiss up the sensitive inside of her thighs. She shuddered, allowing me to press a hand to her stomach and ease her back to the bed.

I moved up, running hands slowly over her body, mouth tasting her, enjoying every sound and sigh.

"Please," she whispered into the quiet.

"Please, what?" Dane asked from behind me. It was his signature question, the one he asked when he wanted to push you to breaking point. He wanted you to tell him exactly what you wanted, what you needed to trip you over the edge.

"I—I—" Blue sounded broken, unsure.

"She wants my mouth on her pussy. Don't you, baby?" I answered for her, giving her an out, knowing it would drive Dane crazy.

"Yes," she purred the word, her hips shifting restlessly.

"Can't speak for yourself?" Dane asked, shifting to the bed.

I looked up, enjoying the view. A naked Dane hovered over Blue, her eyes wide at the sight of his thick, heavy cock.

I may be longer, but the guy had me beat in thickness.

He leaned forward, his face a breath away from hers.

"Answer me, Blue. What do you want?"

Her mouth parted, her little tongue darting out to wet her bottom lip. "A mouth on my clit."

I immediately shifted, my tongue diving into her folds, tasting that which had been forbidden for so long.

Above me, Dane rewarded Blue by kissing her senseless, his hands gently massaging her glorious breasts as I tasted her goodness.

In a satisfyingly short amount of time, her

hips jerked, her body flexing under me as she threw her head back, her body arching up, her pussy flooding my mouth as she came.

"Taste good?" Dane demanded.

I nodded, determined to capture every last drop of her orgasm. When she came back to earth, I slowed, pulling back.

Dane immediately moved to swap places, but not before capturing my mouth in a hard kiss.

"You taste good on his lips," Dane praised, nipping at my mouth.

I shoved him away, chuckling as I moved up to Blue's head. I stretched out beside her, lazily running my fingers up and down her stomach, circling her breasts in light movements. I watched her watching Dane, his head buried between her thighs, his movements deliberate and cunning.

Sure enough, Blue's eyes fluttered closed even as her chest began to rise and fall in quick succession.

"More," she whispered, her hands reaching down to clasp Dane closer to her. "I need more."

Dane liked to tease. He liked to push you to the edge repeatedly before throwing you over in the most beautiful moment of ecstasy.

He must have taken pity on her because her hips bucked once, twice, then she cried out, riding Dane's face, so beautiful and precious in this moment.

Dane lapped at her gently, pressing slow kisses to her inner thighs. "Okay?"

"Perfect," she answered, one arm slung over her face, her breathing still slightly ragged.

"Good," Dane stood, pulling her down the bed until her ass sat on the very edge. "Cause you're gonna suck Drake while I take this little pussy. We're gonna make love to you, baby. You need to stop, you tell us. But until you do, we're gonna make you feel good."

She dropped her arm, her sexy grin going straight to my cock. "Bring it, big boys."

Dane nodded at me, and I moved, crawling up her body to position myself at her head.

We stayed suspended for a moment, all of us on the cusp of our new reality—joined and yet not. Then Blue's mouth opened, and she ran her tongue over my cock.

Fuck. I'm gonna come.

I shut that thought down, trying not to think about how amazing Blue's mouth felt. How wet and hot and perfect. How she took me into her mouth and down her throat. How—

Cold nights in shitty boats, boot camp, that time I had a concussion—I rolled out my 'worst of' list, trying to cool my passions. It worked—barely.

"You ready, honey?" Dane asked from down her body.

Blue answered with a nod and a cute grunt, not even bothering to remove her mouth from around my cock.

Dane eased in, and we both froze. Me watching his thick cock enter her, one agonising inch at a time, Blue trembling between us.

"Baby?" I asked, running a hand over her hair.

She pulled back, my cock popping free. "I'm okay," she breathed out, her eyes drifting shut. "Just...feel so...full."

Dane continued his slow entry, finally bottoming out. I waited, watching Blue adjust. Finally, her hips lifted, and I moved back, watching Dane's face where pleasure warred with concern and a little hope. I got it—hope that we were enough for our girl. Hope she'd stay with us.

Not gonna get away after tonight.

She whimpered, her hands reaching down to Dane, her body now jerking under him. It was all the encouragement he needed. His hips pistoned, his body moving in a hot rhythm designed to tease and tempt her.

"Drake!" she cried, arching her back, reaching out to me. "Need—"

I moved, letting her grasp my cock, letting

her draw it into her mouth and suck it deep down her beautiful throat. I bent over her, my mouth finding Dane's above her, his hands gripping her hips, mine finding her sensitive breasts. We teased our girl, and drove her higher, all while doing the same to each other. This was a night none of us would forget.

"Fuck," I panted as Blue's mouth tightened around my cock, her body's movements becoming more urgent, more desperate.

"Gonna come."

"Together," Dane ordered.

One pump, two. I slid a hand down, fingers finding Blue's slick clit, circling it once, twice—

Her body bowed, her entire being snapping to attention as she came. A gush of moisture coated my fingers.

"Now," Dane grunted, his hips thrusting urgently. "Now."

I let myself go, coming in Blue's mouth. She swallowed, continuing to suck me as Dane came, groaning out his orgasm.

We collapsed on the bed, a tangle of limbs, sweat, and gasps for air. It took long moments to finally calm.

"That was fucking out of this world," I finally said, reaching a hand out to cup Blue's voluptuous ass. "Think you about broke my dick."

"That's a shame," she muttered, her head on Dane's chest.

"Don't worry, he says this every time." Dane pressed a quick kiss to her mouth. "I'll show you how to get him back up."

My cock, the appendage I had thought would never work again, stirred.

"Oh?" Blue asked. "Is it very hard?"

"Only if we do it right."

They both moved, reaching for me. For a moment, I considered protesting. Tonight was meant to be about Blue. But then Dane directed her to sit on my face while he sucked my cock, and I forgot any and all protests.

This is heaven.

5

Blue

In the space of less than twenty-four hours, my entire life had changed. I'd gone from being single, lonely, and feeling a little frumpy to being in a relationship with two men who adored every part of me.

After the marathon sex session, we'd fallen asleep. I'd found myself alternating between being the little spoon with either Drake or Dane or squishing between them. It surprised me that there had been no jealousy. Instead, we'd fallen together in a rhythm I still didn't understand. It felt easy, fun, and somehow deeper—and oh, so right.

I'd woken this morning alone in bed, dragged myself out, and found the guys sitting on the front porch drinking coffee and waiting for cinnamon buns to finish baking.

Dane had pulled me into his lap while Drake went and made me a cup. We'd sat there, chatting about their dreams for their business, for us, for this big house they wanted to fill with memories—and maybe kids.

We ate the sticky warm buns on the porch, the breeze warm, and the sun bright. I thought they'd want to take me back to bed, but instead, they showed me around the property, pointing out all the features and explaining the upgrades.

In the barn, they pressed me into the hayloft, now an additional storage room complete with a beat-up leather couch, and took turns eating my pussy until I had to cry for mercy. I then watched, sprawled across the couch, completely spellbound as Drake and Dane fucked. They knew each other's limits, knew how to stroke, how to press, how hard to move, and what to do to elicit the exact response they needed to come.

And come they did. With me watching, their bodies locked together. They came, and I watched, relishing their pleasure, basking in their love. That love flowed through me, enveloped me, and burrowed its way into the darkest parts of my soul, erasing doubts and engraving this feeling into my core.

I love them.

They were so different. Dane—dark, quiet, and more likely to touch than speak. Though I'd discovered he had no trouble taking control and issuing orders in the heat of the moment. And Drake—light, loud and jovial. He liked to watch as much as he liked to partake, something which had surprised me, considering he was so hands-on and commanding outside the bedroom.

I stared at my phone, struggling to know what to say to my friends.

BLUE

Um… so. I think we need a girls night.

I hit back, deleting the message.

BLUE

I slept with them. And yes, Ani, I will share details.

I hit delete again.

BLUE

Book club Monday. I'll bring the wine.

"There's nothing here." Drake ran a hand

through his hair, the other holding the refriger-ator door open as he peered at the empty shelves.

I hit send on my message and tossed it on the counter.

"I don't understand how you boys ate it all in the few days between me seeing you shopping and today," I finally commented from my seat at their long island, trying to ignore how my heart ached happily in my chest.

"We're growing boys," Drake protested, shooting me a cheeky grin. "Can't expect any food to last around here." He turned back to the fridge. "Case in point."

"Then let's go out," Dane said, exiting the laundry. He hefted the basket up, dropping a kiss on my head as he passed. "Bronze Horseman has a band tonight," he called over his shoulder as he headed outside to the clothesline.

Drake shut the door, moving to lean against the counter. He gave me an eyebrow lift.

I shrugged, "They do have great food."

"And you like dancing," Drake smiled. "You, us, we'll tear up the dance floor."

My heart skipped a little. "Are you sure you want to—" I trailed off, trying to find the words. "Declare like that?"

"Declare you're ours, and we're all together?"

Drake asked, not allowing me to look away. "Baby, we've wanted to do that for years."

The question burned the tip of my tongue, seared through my thoughts, and whispered doubts in my ear.

"Then why did you stay away?"

Drake's eyebrows rose in surprise before settling into a frown, "We should wait for Dane."

I blinked. "You can't just tell me?"

Drake's frown deepened. "It's not that simple."

"Not simple? You just need to tell me why you didn't contact me."

He reached across the island, hooking a hand behind my head. "Babe, just give me two minutes to—"

"Please, Drake. Help me understand."

He blew out a breath. "Fine. You remember when you were eighteen. You had that big shindig planned?"

I remembered. I'd purchased a new dress, done my hair just so, and worked my tail off to ensure it would be my big night, my first as a woman.

They never turned up, despite being on leave.

"We arrived the day before. Were going to surprise you."

I jerked back, blinking rapidly. "But you didn't come to—"

"No." He blew out a breath. "We really should wait for Dane."

I bit my lip, experiencing a million different emotions at once. Finally, I give him a small nod.

"Let's move this to the lounge."

I sat in the one armchair in the room, desperate for space. Drake perched on the couch across from me, his hands clasped between his legs, his gaze trained on me. We heard the door open and Dane's heavy footsteps moving through the house.

"We're in the lounge," Drake called, not looking away from me.

"So, we going—" Dane's voice trailed off. "What's going on?"

"Blue wants to know why we never reached out."

"Fuck." He dropped the basket, reaching two hands up to shove through his hair. "Fuck."

"You're freaking me out," I whispered, glancing from Dane to Drake and back. Dane moved to sit beside Drake, their legs brushing as they exchanged a look.

"First thing," Drake finally said when they'd reached an unspoken agreement. "We've always wanted you. We've always loved you. Even before that night in the garage."

I sucked in a breath, unsure of what to think.

"But," Drake continued. "You were sixteen, and what we wanted, while legal, wouldn't have made sense to anyone but us."

"We didn't want that for you, not at that age," Dane agreed. "High school is shit enough without adding gossip to the mix."

"So, you left?"

"Yeah, but we'd always planned on coming back."

"And we did," Dane said. "The day before your eighteenth."

"But you didn't attend."

"No," Drake agreed. They both looked so sombre, so serious that my heart ached.

"We went to your parents." Drake sighed, shaking his head. "That was a mistake."

"My parents? Why?"

"We asked for their blessing. To date you, to woo you, to marry you."

I blinked in shock. They'd never said a word.

"Your Dad told us no. Your Momma was slightly better, but the final answer was still no."

Dane leaned forward, capturing my attention. "You have to understand, Blue. We grew up without parents. There wasn't any way we were doing something that would have resulted in a breakdown between you and your family."

"Wasn't that my decision to make?"

They shook their heads. "We couldn't have lived with ourselves."

I sat back, sinking into the deep lounge chair, brain whirling. Finally, I looked back over at them, hands gripping the arms of the seat.

"What changed?"

"Your parents."

"What?"

Drake nodded. "Your mother's cancer made them reassess their decision. They called us, we were overseas at the time, but they said they were sorry. Apologized for making a decision that had influenced your life and ours. They realized that we only had your best interests at heart, and we would treat you like the queen you are."

Dane's lips quirked. "I think your mother even said she'd cut our balls off if we ever hurt you."

"But they gave you their blessing?" I asked, my heart thumping loudly in my ears.

"Yeah, baby. Said they'd support us so long as it was your choice."

Tears stung my eyes. "Wow," I murmured, raising a shaky hand to my mouth. "This is— wow."

"We're sorry, Bluebell," Dane said, pinning me with his serious dark gaze. "But we were prepared to live without you if we knew you were happy."

I wanted to rage at them for making this decision without me. I wanted to throw things and rant and make a mess. But I didn't. I let that anger go in a long, hard sigh. Because the fact was, I understood their reasoning. Broken homes, shitty foster houses, they knew the importance of family—particularly a good family —and mine was the best. They wouldn't have done anything to take me away from mine. And as much as I loved both of them, it would have hurt me to have my family reject my decision.

I swiped at my tears, appreciating that they were still giving me the space I needed.

"Is there anything else I need to know?" I asked, finally.

They exchanged a look.

"You get to pick who you wanna marry," Drake told me.

"But the other one gets first chance at knocking you up," Dane growled.

I raised an eyebrow. "Excuse me? You want to marry me?"

"And knock you up," Drake agreed.

They both grinned, and I felt that familiar flutter in my belly.

"What if I want you two to get married?" I asked, genuinely curious.

They looked at each other in surprise.

"But, don't you want a day?"

"Sure, but I can tie myself to you through our babies. You two can't do the same with me. And it doesn't seem fair to only marry one of you."

"How about we decide all this later?" Dane asked, rising to his feet. "You got a choice now, babe. We can either head to the bar or to bed. But either way, you're getting some lovin' first."

I let him pull me up, wrapping my arms around him and settling into his embrace with a sigh. Drake's arms came around us, holding us all together. It felt beautiful. Right.

"Bar," I finally decided. "I want to show off my men."

They both chuckled.

6

Dane

The Bronze Horseman hadn't been here when we'd left Capricorn Cove ten years ago. But then, Ella Bronze had still been in high school back then. Now, she and Anika Sharif, another blast from our past, had built an exceptional venue. Not too big, not too small, the place had a homey but still classy feel to it. They'd added an outdoor area with a small stage for those long summer nights.

We were fast approaching the end of summer, but the heat still hung in the air, and the long afternoon light fell across Blue's face, lighting her in a way I'd only ever dreamed.

We'd eaten, then sat chatting and nursing a few beers while enjoying the warm evening.

She'd turned to watch the band, a satisfied, happy smile on her face. Her body shifted in her seat, her shoulders swaying in time with the hot salsa number.

"You wanna dance?" Drake asked her, his eyes, like mine, dipping to the deep v of her shirt. Her gorgeous tits jiggled as she swayed.

"Love to," she beamed, immediately standing.

I sighed, throwing back the last of my beer and resigning myself to looking foolish as I tried to keep up with these two.

On the dance floor, we sandwiched her between us. My hands falling on her hips, Drake's on her butt. We swayed in time to the music, pressing close, stealing kisses between laughter.

The songs flowed, from one to another, and we were lost in each other. I didn't pay any mind to the looks or whispers; all my concentration was on the beautiful woman before me. Oh, and the guy dancing with her—he wasn't half bad, either.

The band called for a break, and Blue broke away, laughing as she called over her shoulder, "grab me a drink. I gotta pee." She disappeared into the crowd.

"Find us a table. I'll get the beers," I told Drake.

The line moved quickly, Ella working it with precision.

"Hey Dane, welcome back to town." She tilted her head, a genuine smile on her face. "Let me guess, two ciders and a coke?"

"That's it," I agreed. As she handed over the drinks, a shiny piece caught my eye.

"Wow, didn't realise you were married. Congratulations."

She laughed. "Engaged, but we're planning the wedding at the moment. Actually, you guys should meet him. I heard through the grapevine that you fired Simon."

I cocked a brow. "Your guy is into boats?"

"Honey." She leaned forward, a teasing smile lighting her face. "His boats put all others to shame." She reached into her back pocket, pulling free a card to hand me.

"You just keep a stack of these in your pocket?"

She winked as I took it.

"Gotta support my man." She grinned. "But seriously, give Gunnar a call. He and his brother own Thor's Shipbuilding. They've just finished setting up their second workshop down here and are ready to take on new clients."

I lifted the cardboard carton loaded with our drinks. "Cheers, I'll look him up this week."

"Have a nice night, and say hi to Drake for

me." Her smile turned wicked. "And tell Blue I'm looking forward to Book Club."

Before I could ask her what she meant, she turned away, moving to serve the next customer.

I shifted, searching for and finding Drake sitting at a long table, chatting with some guys. He'd snagged the bottom half of the table, three seats along the same side. I placed the drinks on the table, glancing around.

"You seen Blue?"

"Nope," Drake reached for his beer. "You switching?" he asked, nodding to the can of soda.

"Yeah, gotta get your sorry asses home."

He laughed, bumping me with his shoulder. "You get me some chips?"

"Jesus, you're a bottomless pit." I rolled my eyes. "Fine, stay here."

"Order inside; it's quicker," one of the guys at the table helpfully informed me.

"Thanks, be right back," I headed toward the main venue, dodging the milling crowd and nodding greetings to old friends and acquaintances.

Inside, the restaurant was dimly lit, a few tables taken up by couples, but most were outside enjoying the final few weeks of summer. I placed an order and then hit the john before heading back out.

I'd finished and was leaving when I heard Blue's voice cut through the chatter in the long line waiting to use the female toilet. The conversations slowed around me, all turning to listen to the voices carrying from inside the restroom.

"I don't want to hear it, Hannah." Her tone put me on high alert. She sounded colder than ice and madder than hell. I bristled, ready to charge in if needed. I slipped my phone from my pocket, texting a quick message to Drake.

DANE

Inside. Toilets. SOS.

"But," Hannah Sharp's voice sounded stiff. "I'm only trying to give you some advice, honey."

"Okay, one, I'm not your honey. Two, I don't require unsolicited advice about how to keep my men happy. We're ecstatic without your input."

"I have no doubt about that," Hannah replied quickly. "But, you know, it wouldn't hurt to be prepared. Just in case a—" she paused, "— real woman tries to—"

"Whoa," Blue snapped. "Whoa, whoa, whoa. Back the fuck up. Real woman? Who do you think you are, Hannah Sharp? A real woman? As opposed to what? A plastic barbie doll?"

"That's not what I meant—"

Blue cut her off. "Thanks for trying to undermine me, but, unlike you, shitty high school tactics no longer work on me. Bye."

I watched, waiting for my girl to appear. She didn't disappoint. Her hair flowed behind her in a midnight cloud, her tight shirt clinging to every curve, while her denim skirt moulded to her thick thighs in a way that made me want to wrap them around my head.

"Oh," she pulled up, blinking twice at me in the dim light. "Dane, I—"

I caught sight of Hannah over her shoulder as she exited the restroom with a pinched look on her face.

"Yo, Hannah," I called, nodding at her. Hannah's eyes widened, the colour draining from her face. "You ever talk shit to my woman, or, hell, any other woman in town, I will personally see you suddenly need to move. Got it?"

She nodded, her eyes still wide. I felt a touch of satisfaction at the glint of fear I caught in them.

I looked back at my girl. "You good?"

She grinned, crossing her arms, one hip cocked to the side. "I had it."

"I know," I hooked a finger into the pocket of

her skirt, reeling her in. "Doesn't mean I don't need to stake a claim, back you up."

"Caveman," she muttered, letting me fist her hair.

"Fuck yeah," my lips found hers, declaring her mine in front of God, man, and all the gawkers.

"You know," Drake drawled from behind me. "This doesn't exactly look like an emergency."

I chuckled, withdrawing. "Come kiss our girlfriend."

With the gossips still watching, Drake sauntered down the hall, wrapping an arm around me and pressing a kiss to our girl's lips.

"You okay, babe?"

"Perfect," she whispered, beaming at us. "But let's go home. I'm ready for bed."

The way she said bed suggested that sleep was the very last thing on her mind. We pulled away, food forgotten, before heading outside.

The sun had dropped below the horizon, the light now dim in the rapidly darkening sky. Above us, fairy lights twinkled while staff moved about lighting candles and turning on softly glowing mood lamps.

"Actually, let's go to the beach," Drake suggested, guiding us to the truck. "I wanna watch you fuck our girl under the moonlight."

"Oh," Blue pushed her bottom lip out, pouting. "But I wanted to suck you both off."

We froze, the vision of her laving that perfectly pink little tongue over our cocks sending me hard in an instant.

"That," I grunted. "Let's do that."

Drake threw the keys at me, pulling Blue into the backseat of the truck. "Drive, dude."

I grinned, putting the car in gear and twisting to reverse her out. "Just make sure you've got belts on."

"Will do," Drake muttered as he pulled Blue closer, his hands fisting at the back of her shirt, pressing her closer.

We were greedy men. Demanding, forward, and unafraid to declare what we wanted and take it. They made out in the backseat like teens while I drove to a secluded strip of beach. With the sun now completely down, the surfer's beach often became a lover's hang-out for frisky teens. But it was still too early in the evening for them, making it the perfect place for us.

I pulled into a spot just behind the dunes, the night sky large and bright before us.

I got out, rounding the side of the truck to pull open the back door. Blue and Drake were locked in a tight embrace, their clothes dishevelled and their hair a mess.

Hot as fuck.

I reached down, pulling a picnic blanket from under the driver's seat. Drake leisurely wrapped up their make-out session, soothing Blue's protesting whimper with a quiet whisper of assurance that more would come.

Oh, honey. You have no idea

"Come on," Drake commanded, pulling them both out of the truck. "Dane wants a little something too."

Blue looked over at me, her mouth swollen, eyes a little dazed. I fell in behind them, watching in satisfaction as they stumbled in the sand, laughing as they led us down to the beach.

While they kicked sand at each other, I scouted for a sheltered nook, spreading the blanket and settling down to watch.

Blue snatched up a fistful of sand, tossing it at Drake. He roared, dashing at her, gently dropping a shoulder to her stomach and throwing her over his shoulder in a fireman hold.

"Drake!" she shrieked, her dark hair tumbling down, her shirt slipping to reveal the shape of her back, her dark skin beautiful in the moonlight.

The small glimpse broke my control.

"Bring her here."

7

Blue

I shivered at the possessive need in Dane's voice as he ordered us to him. Drake immediately complied, keeping me slung over his shoulder. One hand rested on my ass, rubbing soothing circles as he hauled me across the sand to Dane. Arriving at the picnic rug, he bent, gently putting me down.

I laughed, my hands resting on his shoulders as I shook my head at Drake. "You're terrible."

"And you're adorable," he returned, dropping a kiss to my nose.

"Take off his pants," Dane's rumbled direction sent a hot spear of need shooting straight to my core. I dropped to my knees, feeling the sand shift under me. I twisted, ensuring I would give Dane the best view as I reached for Drake's fly. I felt their eyes on me, watching with heat as I pulled the zip down, revealing the hard outline of Drake's cock pressed against his boxer briefs.

"Oh," I murmured, wanting to tease them both just a little. "What do we have here?"

I slipped my fingers into the band of his briefs, pulling them down along with his jeans. His cock sprang free, thick, heavy, and proud, jutting out at me. I ignored it and instead reached down to help him remove his shoes, and socks then tossed the clothes aside. He let me but got impatient, ripping off his own shirt, and throwing it at Dane who caught it one-handed.

"Lick the tip," Dane ordered, shifting on the blanket to remove his clothes.

I did, just a tiny flick of my tongue against the salty, hot tip of Drake's cock.

"Fuck." Drake's hips jerked, but he remained in place, letting Dane guide us.

"You want him, baby?" Dane's voice was gruff in the warm night air. "You want to suck him? You want that big cock in your mouth?"

I whimpered a little and nodded, my pussy wet, panties soaked. I wanted this, him, them. I wanted a cock in my mouth and one in my pussy—though I'd have settled for either.

"Take him," Dane demanded. "Take him deep."

I surged forward, my mouth wrapping around Drake's cock, searing him with my heat. He groaned, head thrown back, hands coming up to grip the back of my head as I swallowed him down.

"How's our girl feel?"

"Fucking amazing," Drake ran a hand down to cup my cheek. "Looks gorgeous too."

I found my body shifting in a rhythm as old as time, my hips rocking because I needed something, anything, to relieve the thrum of desire between my legs.

Dane moved, his body pale in the moonlight. "I got you, honey."

His hand came up to my hips, and he helped me adjust, moving me into a doggy position. Drake slipped free, and I was about to protest the loss, but he moved to quickly crouch before me, his hands immediately guiding my mouth back to his cock.

Dane hadn't said I could stop. And I knew we were both eager to please him.

I felt fingers hook into the crotch of my panties, finding the slick wetness of my dripping pussy.

"Oh, baby," Dane whispered. "You want this bad, don't you?"

I nodded around Drake's cock, my hips shifting restlessly. "Do you need to be filled, baby? Do you need us both?" I whimpered around the cock in my mouth, my sucking frantic and disjointed. Drake didn't seem to care based on the look of sheer ecstasy on his face. Behind me, Dane's finger traced my lips, teasing me with deliberately light touches.

"Beg for it."

My mouth broke free, and I threw myself back against his hand. "Please!"

"Please what?"

"Please, I need more."

"What do you need?"

"Your cock in me. Drake's in my mouth. Both of you fucking me."

Dane roughly shoved my underwear to the side, his cock finding my entrance. Drake's hand cupped my jaw, guiding my mouth back to his tip. Together they pushed in, breaching my two holes in one agonisingly slow movement. They both swore, fighting for control, but I wasn't having it.

Not this time.

I rocked on my hands and knees, shoving myself forward and backward, taking both of them deeper with each movement.

"Wait, Blue, hold on."

I ignored the protest, wanting them to lose control. Wanting them to fill me, take me, devour me.

"Fuck, give it to her," Dane ordered, his voice a harsh bark in the night.

They did, both fucking me with abandon. I felt it build, heard their whispered praise, listened to them describing how I felt between them, their filthy words driving me higher even as they thrust harder, faster, deeper.

I came apart under them, losing myself in the need to suck and fuck and feel... everything. Cum shot down my throat, and I swallowed even as I felt Dane pull out and cum across my back.

I couldn't describe how fucking hot that was to me. I never thought I'd be a girl who enjoyed being covered in cum, but there I was, incredibly turned on by the thought of him, of them, marking me.

We collapsed on the blanket, panting in the aftermath of our tryst.

"Wow," Drake finally croaked. "That was—"

"Yeah," I chuckled, basking in the warm afterglow.

Dane said nothing, just lay between us, his fingers drawing little patterns on both of our skin.

I finally pushed up, looking out at the crashing waves.

"Don't even think about it," Dane said, his eyes closed.

I pushed out my bottom lip. "You don't even know what I was thinking."

"Any other beach, I'd join you. The surf here is too rough. I'm not dragging your ass out of a riptide."

I raised an eyebrow, a mischievous little part of me bubbling to the surface. "But I thought you were big, brave Marines. Surely you can keep me safe if I'm only up to my knees."

Dane opened one eye, sending me a frown. "Not falling for it."

"But I'm all sticky—"

He sighed, sitting up. "Fine, but only to your knees."

"Promise."

Under the light of the half-moon, the stars looking on, we frolicked in the waves, my two men looking after both my body and my heart —determined to keep me safe.

As we returned to the car, a siren flickered on, screaming into the quiet night as lights flashed red and blue.

"Shit!" I squeaked, slapping a hand over my pubic area and an arm over my breasts. "It's the police!"

I dashed to our car, throwing myself into the back and crouching down. Drake and Dane cackled, both politely cupping their junk but following at a more leisurely pace.

The cruiser stopped, and a police officer climbed out of the driver's seat.

"Dane? Drake? That you guys?"

"Howdy, Sheriff." Dane lifted a hand in greeting. "Nice night for a swim."

I peeked through the window, watching the new Sheriff, Tristan Rodriguez, run a hand through his hair.

"Thought you guys were some rowdy kids I'd have to write up for underage drinking." He quirked his eyebrow, and even in the dark, I could see the amusement on his face. "Looks like it's just for public nudity."

The men laughed while I slid back down in the seat, my cheeks burning with mortification.

"We're just about to head home," Drake explained, nodding at the car. "Gotta get Blue inside before she catches a cold."

I'd gone to school with Tristan Rodriguez. I'd even had a crush on him once upon a time— before Honey admitted she liked him and way before Drake and Dane came on the scene.

Come to think of it, Honey is still single...

"Alright," the Sheriff laughed. "Consider this a warning. You guys have a good night."

He went back to his cruiser, quickly heading off.

Dane and Drake took their sweet time, drying off, dressing, then slid into the front and passenger seats. They both twisted, looking at me over the console, grinning.

"You can both go fuck yourselves," I told them, pulling on my shirt.

"Only if you watch."

I barked out a laugh, then shot them the bird. "I'm angry at you!"

"Nah." Dane twisted back around, putting the car in gear. "But even if you are, I hear make-up sex is hot as hell."

I rolled my eyes but couldn't ignore the little frisson of pleasure that shot through me at that thought.

Hmm—make-up sex here I come.

8

Blue

Ella, Anika, Collins, Honey, and I stood on the footpath staring up at the wreck of my house, watching as a flurry of workers swarmed the ruins of my roof.

Without fail, the Steamy Book Club met every two weeks on a Monday. Over books, booze, and burgers at the closed Bronze Horseman, we bonded becoming a close knit group of phenomenal women who supported each other.

But noting my currently homeless predicament, we'd agreed to pause the book chat in order for us to survey the damage to my house.

"I know it sucks that you're homeless for a little while longer," Honey said, her eyes twinkling. "But the eye candy is totally worth the inconvenience."

A chubby blonde with a big heart, Honey often wore character-themed outfits to book club, and, despite our change of scenery, today was no exception. She wore workman overalls and had a toy chainsaw clipped to her belt, her long hair pulled into two adorable pigtails. She looked like the preschool version of 'My First Tradie'.

She glowed—and not just from happiness. Her pale, pinkish skin burnt easily and in difference to our outdoor location she'd smothered herself in a thick layer of sunscreen.

I'd already caught Anika eyeing her off, no doubt plotting how to draw a penis in the cream.

"Speaking of eye candy." Anika hip-checked me. "How goes it with your delicious men?"

Hilariously dry and irreverent, Anika was one of the most fascinating women I'd ever met. Her long black hair had been tied up in a top knot, and her tawny brown skin held a touch of pink on her cheeks.

She looked happy. Healthy. And far too relaxed for this afternoon.

"You got laid," I said, eyeing her off.

"Twice," she admitted with a happy sigh.

"Mac loves going down on me. The man can't get enough of my dessert."

Collectively we groaned, tossing popcorn, chips and bottle caps at our friend.

"I hate you all," Honey said with a heavy sigh. "Why can't I find a man?"

"Because you want a fairy tale and that takes time." Collins tilted her head my way. "Now, answer the question, Blue. How goes it?"

Collins, a yoga instructor and physical therapist who worked at Honey's health clinic, crossed her arms over her chest, narrowing her rich emerald green gaze on me. Her skin had tanned throughout the summer, offsetting her bronze hair.

I groaned, slumping back against my car. "I love it, but I'm also worn out to the point of chafing. Do you think a vagina can chaff?"

Collins chuckled, crossing her arms over her chest. "You're the nurse, you tell me."

Ella handed me a beer, popping the cap and catching it with one hand in a practised and impressive move. Perfectly abundant, with long curling hair, mahogany locks, and a smile that could kill, I'd never met anyone as at home in their body as Ella.

"It can," she told me with a knowing wink. "Just offer blow jobs or anal instead."

Our group snorted with laughter. Ella's

Viking fiancé was known to be insatiable, and she'd shared many a story of their sexual escapades over the last few months.

I couldn't help but gaze around at the women surrounding me, thankful for their friendship.

"I love you all," I said, wrapping an arm around Ani's shoulders. "Even you."

Anika shoved me, chuckling. "Of course you do. I'm adorable."

One of the workers shouted from their place on top of the roof, the noise ceasing for a moment while they hauled out chunks of the thick tree branch, tossing them to the ground with a heavy thud.

"It's... good," I said softly, watching the tradies work. "It's hard to explain exactly how good it is."

"Try," Honey said, offering me a smile.

I closed my eyes, imagining Drake and Dane were beside me.

"It's like all the pieces of myself that were missing have come back. There's no jealousy or envy. They share freely with me and without me. If one of them wants to make out with me, there's no pressure to do the same with the other. And same for them. We share, but we also separate. It's like no relationship I've ever seen or heard about. It's just..."

"Perfect for you," Ella said with a knowing smile.

"Yeah." I shook my head. "But now I need to work out how to tell my parents. My family is great. Mum and Dad even apparently called Drake and Dane and told them to come back. But it's one thing to do it in theory and a whole other to...."

"Actually see them in your life," Anika finished for me.

"Yeah."

She gave me a little shake. "It's your life, Blue. You get to choose how to live it."

"And if they're half the people I know your parents to be, then they'll love that you're cared for, supported, loved and happy," Honey said firmly.

My heart swelled. "Are you sure?"

Collins nodded. "Absolutely. You should call them now. Tell them."

I mentally did the calculations on timezones and nodded. "Yeah, they should be awake."

Pulling my mobile from my back pocket I sucked in a deep breath and then hit their international calling number. Dad, predictably, picked up immediately.

"Blue? You okay?"

"Hey, Dad." I closed my eyes. "Everything is fine. Is Mum there?"

I heard him move, the phone shuffling between them.

"Blue? What's happening?"

"Am I on speaker?"

"Yes, baby."

I sucked in a deep breath. "Guys, I'm in love."

There was a long pause on the other end of the line.

"That's wonderful, darling," Mum said, sounding amused. "And this couldn't have waited until we returned because...?"

"Because I'm in love with not one man but two."

Honey clasped my hand, giving me a reassuring smile and a warm squeeze.

"And you don't know which one to pick?" Dad asked.

"No, Dad, I—" I laughed quietly. "We're in love together. All three of us. And I want you to be okay with this."

"Blue, are you talking about Drake and Dane?"

"Yes."

My mother sighed heavily down the line. "Oh, thank the gods."

I collapsed back against my car in relief, my eyes drifting shut as I tried to stop tears from falling.

"Baby girl," my father said softly. "We love you. And we'll love whoever you love. We made a mistake years ago and drove off men who were deserving of you. Men we know you loved. You've never been happy without them, Blue. And for that, we're sorry."

"So sorry," my mum whispered, her breath hitching. "Oh, darling. I'm so glad they're back in your life. You deserve nothing but happiness."

We spoke for a few minutes longer then hung up.

"See?" Honey said, brushing hair from my cheek. "They love you."

I nodded, unable to speak.

"Now that's done." She stepped back, holding her arms out wide. "Can we work on finding Collins and me a man or three? I could do with my own personal bordello. They'll have to put up with decorations and my psychotic family but it's a small price to pay for the glory of me."

"You should definitely put that in your dating profile," Anika said with a laugh. She glanced at me. "You good?"

A genuine smile pulled at my lips, lighting my face. "I'm perfect."

"Good." She clapped a hand on my shoulder. "Let's get to the bar. We all need a beer, and

I am dying to talk about that scene with the rope. Did you read that with one hand? I did. I then immediately made Mac go out and buy rope. He said the guy at the warehouse looked at him funny for testing the softness. That author must have done her research because phwoar!"

Chuckling, I tugged open the door to my car and slid in, grateful once again for my incredible life.

9

Drake

I'd never been this nervous in my life. Sweat trickled down my back, and my overly starched collar scratched at my neck.

"Breathe," Dane whispered to me.

The house sat in darkness, waiting for Blue to arrive home. We could hear her come through the door, muttering something about deadlines and dinner reservations. We'd told her to come home early, that we had a birthday surprise waiting.

I suspected she wasn't expecting this.

She opened the door, clicking on the light in the hall. "Drake? Dane? Where are you guys? Why are the lights off—oh."

She must have seen the rose petals we'd laid out on the floor. There was a shuffle, the sound of something scratching against the floor, then her soft footsteps as she followed the roses.

I glanced at Dane, my heart now thumping through my chest. He looked cool as a cucumber, his gaze fixed on the entrance to our bedroom.

We heard her quick gasp, her steps faltering.

She'd moved in a week ago, finally giving in to the inevitable. The damage to Blue's house had been more substantial than initially anticipated, and she'd spent a month in our bed.

When she'd finally returned home, she'd done so despite our wishes, protesting that we needed space and were rushing things.

Instead, we'd moved into her house, sleeping there every night she wasn't at ours. After a month of that fucking nonsense, she'd finally agreed to move in here.

It was step one in our new plan. Tonight, we implemented step two.

I'd spent the day reorganising the house, creating spaces for her things. We wanted Blue to see how easy our integration could be.

The hall she walked down I'd filled with photographs and artwork. I'd removed some of our items, replacing them with hers. We didn't have many shared memories just yet, but we would. If tonight went to plan.

She neared, and Dane's hand came down on my shoulder, squeezing.

"We got this, babe," he whispered to me, his lips brushing the shell of my ear.

I straightened, taking his strength and confidence and projecting it back.

Yeah. We got this.

Blue walked through the bedroom door, pausing just over the threshold. Her eyes were wide and a little dewy as she took in the scene we'd created for her. It had taken an hour, but every damn candle we could find decorated the room, lending it a soft glow.

"Happy Birthday, baby." Dane stepped forward, pulling her into the room.

"My birthday's not 'til tomorrow."

"We know," he replied softly, guiding her to the bed. "But tomorrow is for family. Tonight is for us."

Her lips quirked up in a sexy smile. "I like the sound of that."

Dane shot me a look. I cleared my throat, stepping forward as she settled on the edge of the bed.

"Bluebell McKenney," my voice sounded rough, hoarse, like I was struggling to get the words out.

"Yes, Drake Andrews?" she teased, completely unaware of the magnitude of this situation.

"Will you marry us?" I dropped to one knee, fingers scrambling to find the box, holding out a ring.

Her face froze, her gaze locked on the box.

"Marry—" She looked from me to Dane and back. "But... I thought—"

I coughed, cleared my throat, and then coughed again. Dane took over, sitting beside her, holding her hand.

"We want you, baby. But we also need to keep you safe. We've got no real family, but we want one. Drake can be my next of kin, same with his wife because I've got no one else. But you? Drake? Drake's got family out there somewhere, even if they're shitheads. And you got all your extended. If we have kids? If something happens to you? We need to have access. The only way to do that is to get you hitched."

She looked up at Dane, tears wetting her cheeks. "And you're okay with me marrying him and not you?"

"Honey." He raised a hand, wiping away a tear. "There're no tallies or counting here. We're sharing the bounty of our life." His lips quirked. "But I get first dips on knocking you up."

I finally found my voice, adding, "besides,

Bluebell Andrews sounds better than Bluebell Butler."

She choked out a laugh, finally looking back at me. I swallowed, my normally steadfast sense of composure completely deserting me. I remained on one knee; the ring still held out to her.

"Yes," she finally whispered, her smile gentle. "I want to tie myself to both of you."

I slid the ring on her finger, enjoying the relief that flooded through my veins.

We huddled together, pressing kisses to each other's mouths, enjoying the feel of being together and basking in the joy that tonight had brought.

Finally, with a little sniff, Blue pulled back, her dark eyes dancing with mischief. "Now, can I suck your cocks, or are you gonna make your fiancé wait?"

We didn't make her wait. We feasted on her generous curves, delighted in her feel, relished her cries, and moved together until we all came.

And then we started over again. Because love had no end and no beginning. And for us, this was just one moment in a long line of perfect moments that would be our lives together.

EPILOGUE

Blue

I didn't want to say that pregnancy was a bitch but all evidence said pregnancy was a bitch.

I brushed my mouth for the fourth time that morning, praying the last of my morning sickness had finally dissipated. This was my third pregnancy, but it was definitely going to be my last. Our oldest, Matias, had been born a shade under nine months from our wedding day. He looked exactly like his Daddy, Dane, all dark and broody with a controlling side that came out often. Sofia had come next, Drake's baby girl. She'd inherited his tan skin, blonde hair, and his jovial nature.

This one, though? Twins. We hadn't

planned on any more. Two, and we were done. But then the morning sickness had arrived, and the sonogram had shown two little heartbeats, and I was sure this had to be some kind of dream. But no, with the morning sickness and endless cankles, not to mention the two babies currently tap-dancing on my bladder meaning I had to pee every five minutes, this was very much my reality.

Eight months pregnant and I felt like a whale. I waddled out of the bathroom, finding my men in bed with our two munchkins. Dane handed Sofia over to Drake, exiting the bed to help me get in. I groaned on the way down, my back aching.

"Matt, can you take Sofia and bring us back a book or two?" Drake asked, setting the kids on the floor.

"Yes, Daddy." He pulled Sofia along, telling her, "Daddy is going to read to us."

"But I want Dada," she complained, making grabby hands at Dane.

Our children may look like their biological parent, but there were no lines in this house.

"Bring me back a book, and we'll read it together, sweetheart," Dane told her, blowing her a little kiss. She caught it, making a smacking sound as she stuck it to her lips.

"Ok." She turned, skipping behind her brother as they left the room.

My men immediately turned to me, easing me onto the bed.

"You shouldn't stress yourself," Dane admonished.

"You need to let us help more,'" Drake told me, shifting down the bed to rub my feet. I groaned, eyes rolling back in my head as I felt him knead the sensitive skin. Behind me, Dane began to gently rub my shoulders, letting me lean against him.

This is why you'll go through another pregnancy. You'd do anything for them.

Bringing babies into this house had changed our habits. We still slept together, and still regularly partook of dirty, filthy sex, but our babies had changed our lives. They brought us joy, love, and a new adventure to share together. I'd been worried that they wouldn't be able to love a child that wasn't their own, but my men had proved me wrong. So very wrong. Love, I'd long since learned, had no end or beginning. It simply was. And our love was the very best kind —limitless.

"Mama?" A voice called from the side of the bed. I looked down, seeing my two babies standing with their favourite books in hand.

"Come up here, my pequeños."

Dane reached down, helping them onto the bed. My stomach was so big that they could no longer sit on my lap, but they snuggled into me, small hands resting on my stomach.

"Are the babies awake?" our Sofia asked, her voice filled with wonder.

"Yes, Corazon," I whispered, brushing her hair back from her face. "Would you like to feel?"

"Me too!" Matt called, shifting to place his small hands on the round of my belly.

I closed my eyes, Dane sitting strong and silent behind me, his hands continuing their rhythmic movement while Drake gently directed our babies as our littlest ones kicked inside me.

In this beautiful moment, I felt nothing but overwhelming love.

Thank the gods I took a chance.

I opened my eyes, taking in the beauty of my life.

Sometimes, when you double the D, you get triple the blessings. Lucky me.

Thank you so much for reading Blue, Drake and Dane's story! I hope you loved this triad as much as I do.

If you loved this book, be sure to check out the bonus slice of life on my website!
Next in the Capricorn Cove series is Muffin Top, which features the steamy Sheriff Tristan Rodriguez in his journey for love.

You can continue the entire series by checking them out on my website at
www.EvieMitchell.com
If you enter the code EBOOK10 you can get 10% off your purchase from my website.

ALSO BY EVIE MITCHELL

Capricorn Cove Series

The Shake-Up

Double the D

Muffin Top

The Mrs. Clause

New Year Knew You

Double Breasted

As You Wish

You Sleigh Me

Resolution Revolution

Meat Load

Larsson Siblings Series

Thunder Thighs

Clean Sweep

The X-list

Reality Check

The Christmas Contract

Dogg Pack Books

Puppy Love

<u>Bad English</u>

<u>The Frock Up</u>

<u>Pier Pressure</u>

All Access Series

Knot My Type

Love Flushed

Nameless Souls MC Series

<u>Runner</u>

<u>Wrath</u>

<u>Ghost</u>

<u>Shield</u>

Elliot Security Series

<u>Rough Edge</u>

<u>Bleeding Edge</u>

ABOUT THE AUTHOR

Evie Mitchell is a thirty-something romance author (she/her/hers) living with disability. She believes in inclusion, accessibility, and fierce romance. Her loves include steamy romance novels, her husband, their THREE sausage dogs (heaven help her), and her ever-growing collection of book-related mugs.

As a woman with a diverse work history including in areas such as emergency response, event management, human rights, disability access, and security - her books are filled with true stories (bridezillas), worst-case scenarios (malfunctioning dresses), and her favorite tropes (one-bed).

Evie specialises in fiercely inclusive happily ever afters.